Rita and the Haunted House

KU-453-102

Also by Hilda Offen in Happy Cat Books

Rita and the Haunted House

Hilda Offen

Happy Cat Books

For Georgia Brooks
(who helped me with this book)
and her brother Danny

HAPPY CAT BOOKS

Published by Happy Cat Books Ltd.
Bradfield, Essex CO11 2UT, UK

First published 2004
1 3 5 7 9 10 8 6 4 2

Copyright © Hilda Offen, 2004

A CIP catalogue record for this book is available from the British Library

ISBN 1 903285 91 7

Printed in China by Midas Printing Limited

It was Hallowe'en.

"We're going Trick or Treating with Tania's Dad," said Julie.

"And after that," said Eddie, "we're going to the Parkers'. They're having a Haunted House party."

"Can I come?" asked Rita.

"You'd be scared!" said Julie. "There'll be ghosts!"

"And witches! And monsters!" said Jim.

"Please!" begged Rita.
"No," said Eddie. "You'll be safer here."
"Please! Please! Please!" cried Rita.

"No way!" said Julie; and they shoved the pumpkin on Rita's head and ran off. Rita stumbled round and round in circles and tripped over the cat.

"I'll show them!" thought Rita; and she ran
upstairs and put on her Rescuer outfit.
She looked out of the window.
"Huh! There's Basher Briggs!" she thought.
"Up to no good, as usual."
Basher was disguised as a vampire and he
was frightening old ladies on their way to
Bingo.

Yaargh!

Help!

Rita swooped down and whistled.
Hundreds of rats ran out of the shadows and
surrounded Basher.
"Keep him here!" said Rita. "Make sure he
doesn't move."
Then she was off.

In the next street the Trick
or Treaters were knocking at
a door.
"Trick or Treat!" called Julie.
"Trick!" yelled Basher
Briggs's Grandma and she
hurled a bucket of icy water
over them.

"Time to use my secret Sweet Rays!"
thought Rita. "Here we go!"
The water froze in mid-air. Then it turned
into a shower of sweets and fell to earth.
"Hooray!" cried the Trick or Treaters.
"Thank you, Rescuer!"
Rita flew on. She'd heard a strange sound.

Some big green monsters were knocking at a window. Every time the Turner family looked out the monsters pulled horrible faces and roared "Boo!" The Turners were in a panic.

Rita crept round to the back door.
"Let me in!" she called through the cat-flap.
"I'm here to help."
"Are we glad to see you,
Rescuer!" gasped
Mr Turner.

Rita marched up to the window.
"Open the curtains!" she said. "Now!"
"BOOOO!" she roared as the curtains
swished back.

14

"Aargh!" squealed the monsters. "It's the
Rescuer! Let's get out of here!"
And they charged away into the distance.
"Oh, thank you, Rescuer!" cried Mrs Turner.
"Have a toffee-apple!"
"Thanks!" said Rita. "But I think I'm
needed in the park."

15

"Hoooo! Woof-woof! Hooo-ooo!"
A little werewolf had caught his tail in the
slide. Rita untangled him and he slid down.
"Boo-hoo!" he whimpered.
"What's the matter?" asked Rita.

"I wish I wasn't a werewolf!" he snuffled.
"I'm a boy in the daytime but at night I
have to run around scaring people.
I don't like it. I get really lonely."

"Watch this!" said Rita. "Don't take your eyes off it."
She swung her belt buckle backwards and forwards and she spoke very slowly.
"You - will - give - up - werewolfing," she said. "From - now - on - you - will - be - an - ordinary - boy."

She snapped her fingers and the werewolf
turned back into little Joey Harper.
"Come on," said Rita. "I'll see you home."

Rita dropped Joey at his house.
"Hallo!" she said. "What's all that screaming
coming from next door?"

A ghost was on the loose in the Haunted
House - and what was worse, it was a real
ghost!
Everyone was terrified. The ghost floated
round the room, flapping its arms and
wailing "Whooo!"
Rita jumped through the window.

"Can't catch me!" said the ghost.
"Whoooo-ooo!"
"We'll see about that!" said Rita.
The ghost floated through a wall; and so
did Rita. Then it floated through the
ceiling; and Rita followed it.

"Whoooo-hoooo!" wailed the ghost
and it shot up the chimney;
but Rita was close behind.

Rita chased the ghost round and round the
chimney-stack until at last the ghost
collapsed in a heap and gasped, "I give up!
You win!"
"Then off you go!" said Rita. "And keep
going."
The ghost gave a shriek and flew away; and
it didn't stop until it reached the moon.

"Kitty, Kitty, Kitty!"
Julie was stroking a cat.
"I wonder who you
belong to?" she said.
She soon found out.
A witch swooped down
on her broomstick.

She snatched the cat in one hand and
Julie in the other and streaked off
through the night sky.
"We'll be late for the witches' party!" she
cackled.
"I'm not a real witch!" screamed Julie.
"Let me go!"
But the witch took no notice.

Me-ow!

OW!

Rita zoomed after them. She grabbed
the broomstick and shook it.

The witch fell into
a holly bush and
her cat fell on top
of her.

Rita caught Julie and flew her back to the
Haunted House; and she performed some
amazing feats on the way.
Rita parked the broomstick by the front door.
"Boo-hoo-hoo!"
The sound was coming from the front room.
"What's going on here?" asked Rita.

Can I have your auto-graph?

Sorry – I'm needed indoors.

"I was telling them a story," said Mr Parker.
"And they started to cry. We'd just got to the
bit where the big red-eyed monster jumps
out of a cupboard."

"BOO-HOO!" roared the children, more
loudly than ever. Rita raised her hand and
they stopped. "Don't be scared!" she said.
"Everything was alright in the end - because
I came along!"

The children smiled and started to clap.
"Oh - thanks, Rescuer," said Mr Parker.
"Would you like to stay for some apple-bobbing?"
So Rita did; and she just had time to judge
the fancy-dress competition before she went
home.

First Prize goes to the pumpkin!

By the time the others came back Rita was
in her pyjamas.

"Look, Rita - we've brought you a toffee-
apple!" said Eddie. "And some vampire
teeth."

"You missed the Rescuer again!" said Jim.
"She was fantastic! She stopped us from
getting soaked."

"She chased away a ghost!" said Julie. "And
she saved me from a witch."

Rita licked her toffee-apple.

"Did she?" she said. "She must be really,
really brave."

Rita in Wonderworld

Abandoned in the Chicks' Nest Play Area, Rita doesn't find Wonderworld much fun. Luckily she has her secret outfit to hand – soon she is tightrope walking, chasing gorillas and rescuing her brothers from a giant spider's web.

Rita and the Flying Saucer

When a flying saucer lands on earth with a group of aliens from planet Norma Alpha on board it's time for Rita the Rescuer to call on all her special powers. She smashes an asteroid, takes a lost Norm back to the flying saucer and even shows the visitors the quickest way home.

Roll Up! Roll Up! It's Rita

Rita's family thinks she is too small to dress up for the school fair. But Rita has her own special Rescuer's costume and in the blink of an eye she is saving a hot-air balloon, rounding up sheep and winning the tug-of-war single-handed!

Arise, Our Rita!

Rita may be the youngest of the Potter family, but she also is the fabulous Rescuer! And teaching archery to Robin Hood, taming dragons and giants, is all in a day's work for our pint-sized superhero.